This Book Belongs To:

. . . .

For Kelly

So you'll always
remember you
came from a long
line of storytellers.

the GREAT flying RANGER

written by Kathy Campbell

illustrated by Marla Pedersen

Hickory
Dickory
Dock
Place under
Your pillow
A dirty old sock,
That's what you can do
To fall asleep

Or would
You rather
A story
I've got one
That's neat!

See, this guy
Spidey Kidity
Got himself in a mess
And his friend ...

Pinchy Winchy
Was with him...
I guess.

Not to mention
Their buddy
A cross eyed kook
Who insists
That his name
Is cranky ol' "Luke!"

These three
Like to hike
On back roads
Unknown
Walking in circles
Looking for gnomes
It's quite a fun hobby
If you like to
High climb
But I'll tell you all
About it
At another
Bedtime

They walked
And they walked
Until
They stopped
In their tracks

Seems they hit
A rock wall
Or was it
Stones in a stack?

Their eyes moved
On upward
At the end
Was a shock!

What they saw
Left them speechless
They all
Could not talk!

The GIANT was drooling
He liked Spidey
The best!

So these guys
Took off running
To the top
Mountain crest.

Pinchy started crying
He was really upset
And I'm sure
Luke was swearing
If I were to bet!

When who should appear
In the midst of this danger
But the FANTASTIC!
DYNAMIC!

THE GREAT FLYING RANGER!

He was flying back and forth,
Swinging his
Magic lasso
In a tiny
Red plane
I hear he
Bought in
Paso

This Ranger's quite slick
I just have to boast
I've seen him rope cattle
While eating burnt toast.

He's a jack-of-all trades
And a master of some
Cooking for royalty
But, that was for fun.

His secret true love
Is a 747
Which I think he will fly
When he goes up to Heaven.

But, back to my story or you may fret
I do tend to ramble but I'll never forget...

How he swooped
Down upon them
Twirling that amazing
Trick rope
And we all watched
In awe
We all watched
With hope!

He's a fast flying thinker
How he managed that oaf
He just dangled
An edible, incredible
Homemade
Meatloaf!

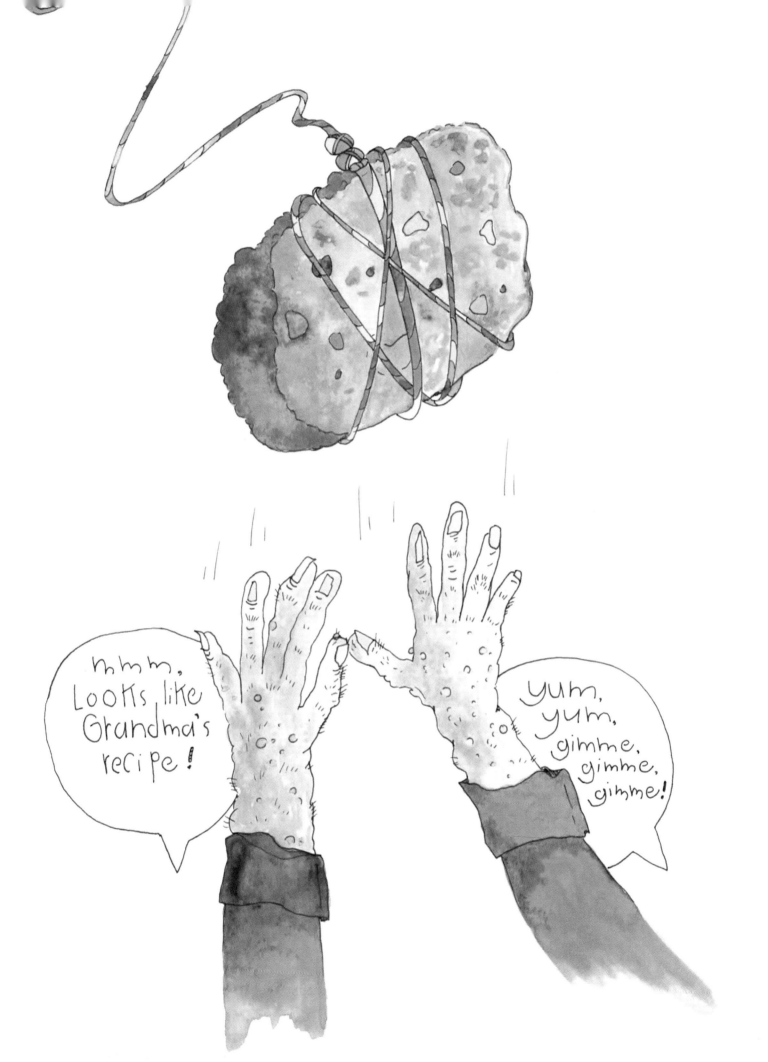

Giants are so silly
And they never quite look
As that rope changed on over
To a huge
Mighty hook!
The Ranger then whisked him
Off to Candy Cane Land
And I know I'll never see
Anything handled
So grand!

Well, that is my tale
Or call it a rhyme.
I hope you enjoyed it,
I had a nice time!

But,
Just between us
I know a bit more
That I think I'll confide
Before
Ending this lore.

I was there by myself
Hiding up on a hill,
And I saw the whole thing
From a windowless sill.
I was in my tree fort
The one with two doors
When I was struck
With the knowledge
Of a whole lot
And more!

See,
That
Rangers
No
Stranger.
I 'bout fell from
My pad!
To my startled amazement...

Kathy Campbell

Kathy grew up in the San Francisco
Bay Area listening to her airline
pilot father, John, tell wild stories
on long car drives. She blended
these funny little stories for her daughter,
Kelly, to enjoy and share as the years
go by. Kathy spends most of her time
with her boyfriend, Len, and presently
lives in beautiful Petaluma, California
with her dog named Bob.

Marla Pedersen

Marla is an art teacher for all ages and
an artist, known for her illustration style
and hand drawn type. She also illustrates
books for all ages, with *The Kind Self-Healing Book*,
written by Amy Eden, as her first published work.
Marla lives and works in Petaluma, California
with her husband and two boys. Discover
more of her work on her website and
social media. www.ripplestudio.net
and instagram.com/marlapdrsn

Made in the USA
Las Vegas, NV
18 December 2020